Three Blind Mice

Retold by
Stephen Cosgrove

Illustrated by
Wendy Edelson

IDEALS CHILDREN'S BOOKS
Nashville, Tennessee

Published by Ideals Publishing Corporation
Nelson Place at Elm Hill Pike
Nashville, Tennessee 37214
ISBN 0-8249-8272-X

Dedicated to Robert, Michael, and René,
the original three blind mice.

Stephen

Once upon a time, there was a house, a pretty house, upon a hill. In this house there came to live a mouse and a mouse and a mouse. One, two, three. Can you see?

Now these mice that moved into this house were blind, so they couldn't see you or me.

To be pitied? No! For these were special mice, these three blind mice that wanted to live in this house.

One of the mice, simply spoken just a mouse, that moved into this house was named Alfred. Alfred played a harmonica all of his life. He could even play a flute called a fife. Alfred was one of the three blind mice.

Another mouse that moved into this house was called Missie. Missie could dance and glide like she was sliding on ice. She would spin and twirl not once, but twice. Missie was one of the three blind mice.

The last mouse that moved into this house was simply called Moe. Moe was as strong and fast as he could be. He could even run faster than a bumblebee. Even he was one of the three blind mice.

Now, the problem you see was that this house was really owned by a farmer's wife. She loved her house and she loved her life. What she didn't like was mice or any mouse in her house.

So, now the story of a farmer's wife and . . . three blind mice.

Three blind mice,
Three blind mice,
See how they run,
See how they run.
They all run after the farmer's wife, who drops
from her hand the butter knife. Have you ever
seen such a sight in your life . . . as three blind
mice?

Three blind mice,
Three blind mice,
See how they play,
See how they dance.
They tickle and giggle the farmer's wife. She dances around to the sound of a fife. She has never laughed so much in her life . . . as with those three blind mice.

Three blind mice,
Three blind mice,
See how they laugh,
See how they sing.
They live a good life with the farmer's wife, who
plops jam on their bread with a butter knife,

Have you ever seen such a sight in your life . . .
as those three blind mice?

About the Author

In 1973, Stephen Cosgrove stumbled into a bookstore to buy a fantasy book for his daughter but couldn't find one that he really liked. He decided he was looking for something that hadn't been written. "I went home and that night I wrote my first book."

Since that fledgling effort over a decade ago, Cosgrove's books have sold millions of copies worldwide.

Cosgrove was born in 1945. He attended Stephens College for Women in Columbia, Missouri ("A great year but I learned little and forgot a lot"), is married, and lives on a quiet little flower farm in Redding, California. There he writes on his computer, communicates by telefax with eight children's book illustrators about current projects, and takes healthy breaks to play with the dog and pick the daisies.

Titles In This Series

Billy Goats Gruff
Goldilocks
Humpity Dumpity
Three Blind Mice